FRANKLY, FRANNIE

Miss Fortune

by AJ Stern

illustrated by Doreen Mulryan Marts

Grosset & Dunlap
An Imprint of Penguin Group (USA) Inc.

For Frances Eder, who kept me on task until
the very last word was written. It was my great fortune
to have had her by my side—AJS

Thanks as always to everyone at Penguin: Francesco Sedita, Bonnie Bader,
Scottie Bowditch, and my editor, Jordan Hamessley, and also, of course,
to Doreen Mulryan Marts, who draws Frannie just like I'd pictured her.
Your support and enthusiasm is unparalleled! To Julie Barer, who negotiates like
nobody's business and to my family and friends for support. Special thanks go to
Esther and Richard Eder in whose house I wrote this and to Frances Eder whose
daily word count check-ins became my favorite time of day. Thanks to Luke Eder for
introducing me to the island of Vinalhaven, where I wrote this book. And of course to
my nieces and nephews: Maisie, Mia, Lili, Adam, and Nathan, without whom I'd have
lost touch long ago with the bane and beauty of kid linguistics. —AJS

GROSSET & DUNLAP
Published by the Penguin Group
Penguin Group (USA) Inc., 375 Hudson Street, New York, New York 10014, USA
Penguin Group (Canada), 90 Eglinton Avenue East, Suite 700, Toronto,
Ontario M4P 2Y3, Canada (a division of Pearson Penguin Canada Inc.)
Penguin Books Ltd., 80 Strand, London WC2R 0RL, England
Penguin Group Ireland, 25 St. Stephen's Green, Dublin 2, Ireland
(a division of Penguin Books Ltd.)
Penguin Group (Australia), 250 Camberwell Road, Camberwell, Victoria 3124,
Australia (a division of Pearson Australia Group Pty. Ltd.)
Penguin Books India Pvt. Ltd., 11 Community Centre,
Panchsheel Park, New Delhi—110 017, India
Penguin Group (NZ), 67 Apollo Drive, Rosedale, Auckland 0632, New Zealand
(a division of Pearson New Zealand Ltd.)
Penguin Books (South Africa) (Pty.) Ltd., 24 Sturdee Avenue,
Rosebank, Johannesburg 2196, South Africa

Penguin Books Ltd., Registered Offices: 80 Strand, London WC2R 0RL, England

Text copyright © 2012 by AJ Stern. Illustrations copyright © 2012
by Penguin Group (USA) Inc. All rights reserved. Published by Grosset & Dunlap,
a division of Penguin Young Readers Group, 345 Hudson Street, New York, New York 10014.
GROSSET & DUNLAP is a trademark of Penguin Group (USA) Inc. Printed in the U.S.A.

Library of Congress Control Number: 2011031481

ISBN 978-0-448-45748-2 (pbk)   10 9 8 7 6 5 4 3 2 1
ISBN 978-0-448-45749-9 (hc)   10 9 8 7 6 5 4 3 2 1

ALWAYS LEARNING   PEARSON

CHAPTER

My mom was throwing a surprise party for my father's fortieth birthday. I was **not allowed** to tell one person in the entire world about it, and I did not. I only told my best friend, Elliott. And Millicent. And Elizabeth, but only just a **smidge**. I didn't even tell her the entire secret. Just the part about the surprise. And the party.

When you have a surprise to keep secret, you need to have very good control over your mouth. A for instance of what I mean is that your mouth wants to yell, "WE'RE HAVING A SURPRISE PARTY FOR YOU, BUT I'M NOT SUPPOSED TO TELL!!!" at your father when he walks in the door from work. But you can't, so instead you say, "Guess what, Dad?"

And he says, "What, Birdy?" (It's a scientific fact that my dad calls me Birdy because that is my middle name, but please don't tell anyone about that fact.)

And your mom gives you a "Don't you dare spoil the surprise" stare from across the room.

And you say, "Elliott was born on Swiss Cheese Day!"

This day is January 2, and you can even look it up if you don't believe this scientific fact. My teacher, Mrs. Pellington, had been teaching us about commemorative holidays. Those are special holidays where you celebrate things that aren't Christmas.

And he grabs and squeezes you and kisses you on the top of your head and says, "Is that a fact?"

You do this because if you don't fill your mouth up with holiday facts you might slip and say something at dinner like, "Who do you think will be at the party?" Or, "What kind of cake will we have?" Or even, "Will there be live music?"

You have to try your very hardest to pretend that nothing exciting and new is going to happen in your life. That nothing is **dancing and tickling** the inside of your brain. You have to be a very talented actress and act like there is NOTHING inside your skull that wants to explode into words outside of your mouth that say: "WE'RE GOING TO HAVE A SURPRISE PARTY FOR YOU, DADDY!!!"

The best part about the party was that my mom was going to have a fortune-teller. I was so **excitified** by this news, my ears almost fell off when she told me.

If you don't already know this about fortune-tellers, they tell you about yourself later in life.

A for instance of what I mean is that one might look at me right now and say, "Frances B. Miller, when I look into your future, I see a **gigantorous** office with the hugest desk right in the center. A very professional-looking assistant works for you. You have an office supply closet with fresh-smelling legal pads and boxes of binder clips and folders with many pockets."

This would be a fortune about my future that I would really prefer. This is because I am very interested in jobs and offices, and I really need an assistant. I asked my parents for one. They're thinking about it.

One thing I wasn't sure I would like about being a fortune-teller was that they didn't have offices. That's why I decided I was going to be an office fortune-teller. This means that I would go to people's offices to tell their fortunes.

I would **certainly and however** need an assistant for this. I would have my assistant carry and open up all the fortune cookies that we had to read to our customers.

I did not know where I was going to get all those fortune cookies, though. When I asked my mom about this, she said that's not how fortune-tellers work, **apparently and nevertheless**. Then I saw her face get an idea. "But," she said, "fortune cookies might be a really fun thing to order for the party!"

What fortune-tellers do, actually, is tell your fortune using things that are not fortune cookies. The fortune-teller my mom hired looks at cards to read your future.

I have a lot of cards, too: Uno, Go Fish, Old Maid, and regular playing cards. If I had known you could see people's futures in the cards, I would have looked much more carefully.

My mom told me that the fortune-teller could also stare at your palm and tell your fortune by looking at all the lines. I've looked at all the lines on my palm before, and I can tell you for a scientific fact that I've never seen my future there.

Fortune-telling was a career I was very interested in having, but because I could not see my future in cards or palms, I was worried I was not going to be a **natural** at this job. I like to be a natural at things. Maybe the fortune-teller would give me special tips.

The party was not for another two entire days, which meant I had to wait, which is a for instance of something I do not like to do.

I tried doing distractifying things like hula-hooping. I jumped around on one foot. I made more business cards in case I needed to hand them out at the party and also worked on my résumé (which is a list of all the places you've worked).

Then I called Elliott, but he couldn't talk because he was practicing for the big music recital on Tuesday night. He plays the clarinet, and he is very good. That is why I told him he didn't need

to practice and *could* talk to me on the phone. He disagreed and said he'd call me later.

This is not a sentence I prefer. It is a scientific fact that while time does pass, it does not pass *faster* when you are waiting for it to pass faster. The only way that the party would get here was to wait. That's what my mom said. So that is what I did. I waited.

CHAPTER

Because the party was at our house, my mom had to figure out a way to set up without my dad around.

My mom is very **geniusal** because she came up with the best plan my **ear sockets** had ever heard. My dad's college roommate, Simon, was flying in from Chicago to be at the party. He was staying at a nearby hotel with his wife. My mom arranged for Simon to call my dad a week in advance to say that he was passing through Chester on business. Did we all want to get together on Saturday and maybe go into New York City?

My mom pretended she didn't know anything about this plan and acted very **excitified** when my dad told her.

It was decided that on Saturday me, my mom, my dad, Simon, and his wife would go to New York City to do some sightseeing.

That is when things got **geniusal**. Because I am a really good actress, my mom gave me a very big part in the surprise party planning play. On Saturday morning, I was going to wake up and pretend I was sick (I am really good at this and that's not an opinion). Then my mom was going to say she had to stay home with me and my dad should just go with Simon.

After my dad asked my mom eleventeen times whether it was *really* okay if he went without us, he finally decided that my mom meant it when she said, "Yes, Dan. It's REALLY okay. I want you to go and have fun."

And that is what happened. When my dad drove off, I jumped out of bed and my mom hired me for a lot of jobs. She didn't even have to look at my résumé or my business cards. She knows I'm a very serious worker.

My first job was to wipe down all the tables so that they shined. My second job was to put mixed nuts in little bowls and put them out in different places. My third job was to answer the phone and tell the person my mom would call them back. My fourth job was to show the person with the big bag of fortune cookies where to go. And my fifth job was to go to my room and finish my dad's present.

My present was homemade business cards, which I was making the same way I made mine: out of a Kleenex box. I was almost done but had a few more to go. His said:

DANieL Miller
40 years old.
Very hard worker
212-414-3745

Before long, my mom yelled up that it was time to get dressed. I pulled out my party dress that my mom said I *had* to wear, even though I am not really a dress type of person. I got dressed and brushed my hair, and as I raced downstairs, the bell rang. The first party guest!

"Frannie, will you get that, please?" my mom yelled.

I ran to the door and opened it. There was a woman with very long, brown hair wearing jeans, a sweatshirt, and sneakers.

You will never in seventy hundred years guess who it was. *The fortune-teller.* She did not look at all how a fortune-teller was supposed to look.

All my sadness slipped down myself and splashed into a big

disappointment puddle on the floor. In one hand she was holding a small suitcase.

"You must be Frannie," she said. I could not even believe what an amazing fortune-teller she was! She didn't even have to ask me my name. She just knew it off the top of her brain. I guess you didn't have to LOOK like a fortune-teller to be a really amazing one.

"I'm Star," she said.

Star.

Wow.

That was the most **fortune-tellerish** name I'd ever heard. I wanted a fortune-teller name, too.

"I'm going to need a lot of help. You seem like the type of person who loves jobs. Is that true?"

I couldn't even talk I was so

impresstified. I nodded and hoped that my mouth wouldn't fall off my face.

"Excellent, because I need an assistant. Are you available to work for me?"

"Yes," I said, very **seriousal**.

"Great. You're hired!" Star told me.

Those were the most beautiful words my ears had ever heard.

"Your first job is to introduce me to your mom so I know where to start setting up."

"Okay," I said, finding my voice. "I know where she is, actually. Follow me," I told Star, leading her into the kitchen.

My mom was a really good baker, and she was making my dad the best cake in the **entire worldwide world**. It was chocolate with two very thin homemade strawberry jam layers inside. This was her specialty and my dad's favorite.

"Mom, this is Star," I told her. "She's the fortune-teller, and I'm her assistant!"

My mom smiled at Star.

"I am so pleased to meet you," my mom said, shaking her hand. "I've heard wonderful things about you." My mom always said the most **rightful** things to people.

"Where shall Frannie and I set up?" Star asked.

That's when I looked at Star with my most **seriousal** face. I didn't know if I should use my English accent or not. That's what I use when I'm being very **seriousal**.

"You can call me Frankly," I said in my regular voice. "That is my professional name."

"Very well, Frankly. Let's follow your mother and set up our office, shall we?"

That is when my head almost fell off my body. How did Star know simply every single thing about me that I loved? And also, an office? We were going to set up an office?

This was going to be the best surprise party I'd ever been to, even if it was the only one I'd ever been to.

CHAPTER

Star's office was a folding table and two folding chairs. She put the chairs on either side of the table so they were facing each other.

I made a **brain note** to get a folding table and two folding chairs.

When she laid a very bright, twirly-colored tablecloth on top of it, I made a brain note to get a very fortune-telling type of tablecloth.

She then pulled out a box of cards

and set them off to the side. Those were the cards my mom told me about. Next she took out a writing pad and a pencil and set it across from her. When she was finished, she asked if I would show her to the bathroom.

While I waited for her to come out of the bathroom, I studied her office. I was very curious about her deck of cards because they did not look like the ones I had. A for instance of what I mean is that on the box there was an illustration of a king on his throne holding more than one sword. I did not realize that people held more than one sword at a time.

When Star came out of the bathroom I hardly even recognized her. She was wearing a red, shiny dress with a scarf wrapped around her waist. Her hair was pulled back into a **lowish** sort of bun, and she was wearing a beautiful, shiny scarf like a headband. She had lots and lots of necklaces. Too many to count. And a lot of bracelets, too. She was wearing bright-red lipstick and her cheeks were pink and her eyes had a lot of black around them. She looked very spooky and very **fortune-tellerish**. That is when I told Star I'd be right back and ran to my mom.

"Can I put on a red dress?" I asked her.

"I don't think you have a red dress, Frannie," she said.

"Frankly," I corrected her.

"Sorry, Frankly."

"Can I get a red dress?" I asked.

"Yes, but not today, love."

"Okay," I said and ran back to Star

who told me to sit across from her and she would show me the cards.

"These cards are very special," she explained to me. "They're called tarot cards, and each one tells a different story. When someone picks their cards, they have picked their story."

I wasn't sure I understood completely, but I nodded, anyway.

"This is the ten of cups. Do you see that there is a very loving family pictured?" She held up the card, and it was actually very true, so I nodded. "This means the person who picks this has a good family life. If they *don't* have a good family life right now, they will. They just need to be patient."

This was the most interesting job I'd ever had in my entire life.

"What does this one mean?" I asked,

pointing to one that looked a little bit scary. Two people were walking with their heads down in the snow, and they did not look very happy about that fact.

"That is the five of pentacles. It means that a person might have some failures and losses. It indicates an obstacle."

Then Star told me what my **exact** job would be. My job was to bring people over, one by one. The people had to look like they needed their fortunes read.

"How will I know who needs one?"

"Well, that's up to you. You'll have to rely on your instincts," Star told me.

"What are those?"

"The feelings you get in your gut that tell you when something is right."

I smiled at her really big because I knew exactly what she was talking about. Sometimes when it was time to pick out a book during reading hour at school, I knew exactly which book I wanted to read.

I **jumped up** when the doorbell rang and ran to get it. Another of my jobs was letting people in, which is the exact thing I did. I could not wait until my dad got here and we got to all yell "surprise" at his face.

Before I even knew it, the entire living room was all filled up and my mom came running in with an excited, red face and cried, "Simon just called. They're coming!"

I was so excited I started giggling and had to cover my mouth. My mom turned out all the lights in the living room and everyone was shushing one another, and then we heard the sound of a car coming down the driveway. When it stopped, the car doors opened and slammed.

We were very quiet. Someone coughed and someone else said, "Shh." It was **extremely suspenseful**, and that is not an opinion. It was also the most exciting moment of my entire life.

I heard my dad's voice outside and his keys jangling. If I got even an inch more excited, I would probably explode.

The door opened and I heard my dad say, "I wonder where they could have gone."

"Beats me," Simon said. "Why don't you show me around?"

My dad's footsteps grew louder and closer, and when he flipped on the lights, we screamed at the top of our guts, "SURPRISE!"

My dad gasped and jumped. Then he put his hand on his heart, and Simon put his arm around my dad's shoulders and gave him a side hug.

"Surprise, dear friend."

My dad's face was the **reddest-red** I've ever seen it. It almost matched Star's dress.

"I can't believe it!" he said.

Then my mom and I ran up to him and hugged and kissed him, and the whole room started to clap and sing "Happy Birthday" together.

The party hadn't even started, and so far it was the best party I'd ever been to **actually and nevertheless**.

CHAPTER

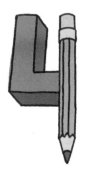

My job as Star's assistant was one of the best jobs I've ever had in my life, and that is not an opinion.

I was very good at using my guts. Star even said so, based on the very first person I brought to her. Star let me stand close and said I could listen, but I wasn't allowed to speak or hover. That meant she didn't want me to accidentally breathe in her **magical powers** because then I'd have them, too.

The first person I brought to her was a friend of my mom's named Rosemary. Star asked Rosemary whether she would like her palm read or her fortune told from the cards. Rosemary chose the cards, and Star told her to shuffle them.

While she was shuffling, Star asked Rosemary to think of a special question she wanted answered. When she was done, she asked Rosemary to divide the deck into three piles. While she was doing that she should still think about her question.

I made a **brain note** of all of this. When Rosemary was done, Star said it was time for Rosemary to ask her question out loud.

"Will I be a famous artist?"

Then Star turned over some cards

and did a lot of *hmmm*ing and *ah-haa*ing. Then she turned over more cards and *hmm*-ed and *ahhh*-ed some more.

Finally, when she had about nine cards laid out, she told Rosemary the story of what the cards said.

A for instance of what I mean is that she pointed to the first card and said, "This card represents your past. In the past, you encountered a lot of obstacles. This card represents who you are now," and then she explained to Rosemary who she was right then.

Star said something about having difficulty and keeping your eyes open for the unexpected. Then she said something about jobs that were not good and she should leave and get a new one. Then she turned over some more cards and told more and more about Rosemary's future.

There were so many different cards, and each one had a special name and meaning. It was a lot to take **brain notes** about.

When they were done, Star stood up and said, "This concludes our reading."

That's when I reached into the fortune cookie bag and gave Rosemary a cookie.

I looked at Star, and she winked at me, which meant she thought giving a fortune cookie was a very **fortune-tellerish** thing to do.

Rosemary took the cookie, thanked Star, and told everyone how fabulous her reading was. I went to find someone else, and this time I brought back Elliott's mom, Julie.

"I want to know if I will ever find love again," she asked Star and then stuck her palm out for her to read. I was very happy about this because I had no **brain notes** about palm reading.

Elliott's parents had just gotten divorced, which was very sad. His dad had a girlfriend already, but Julie did not have a boyfriend. This is a for instance of why she wanted to know about getting one.

The palm reading went something like this: "You have a very strong heart line. It intersects with your life line. You may not feel like you have much luck in love, but you are wrong. The second part of your life is much better than the first. You will meet the man of your dreams sooner than you might expect."

"Really?" Julie asked, getting red in the face.

"Yes. Brace yourself now. I also see a wedding in your near future."

"A wedding?"

"Yes. You will be getting married again. Now, let's take a look at your health line."

There were a lot of lines on the palm that I had to remember. I tried to repeat them over and over so I wouldn't forget: heart, head, health, life, marriage, money, fame. Heart, head, health, life, marriage, money, fame. Heart, head, health, life, marriage, money, fame.

At the very end of the reading, Star looked Julie right in the **eye sockets** and said, "You are going to be exceptionally happy."

Then she stood up and said, "This concludes our reading."

Then I handed her a fortune cookie, and she nearly danced away, that's how filled up with **happiness** she was.

The party went really late, and my parents let me stay up. But the best part was that before it was over, they let Star give ME a reading. I already knew what my question was, and I thought about it while I shuffled the cards. Then, when she laid them all out, she asked me to tell her what I wanted to know.

"Will I have my very own office when I grow up?" I asked her.

The card reading went very well because apparently, I am not only going to have my own office, I'm going to be the BOSS of at least three people. I could hardly believe my **ear sockets** I was so **excitified** by this news.

However and nevertheless, the last cards I turned over were not as good.

"You often act before you think, and that gets you into a lot of trouble," she told me.

My mom, dad, and I looked at one another, shocktified because this was a scientific fact.

"You have a very active imagination, and you can get lost in your own fantasies. You must learn how to control this." Then she stood up and said, "This concludes our reading."

After Star left, my mom, dad, and I all took fortune cookies and read one another our fortunes. My mom went first: "A thrilling time is in your immediate future."

"Your greatest fortune is the large number of friends you have," my dad read.

"Hey, that's a good one!" my mom said. Then it was my turn. When I opened it, I got **chilly bumps** all over my skin top.

"Your many hidden talents will become obvious to those around you."

I knew exactly what this fortune meant. It meant that I *did* have hidden talents as a fortune-teller. Hidden talents should not go to waste, and that is why I decided that I was going to open my very own fortune-telling business at school.

CHAPTER

I spent the entire day on Sunday getting ready to open my fortune-telling business.

First, I found a deck of playing cards, but they didn't have pictures on them like Star's did. So I decided to make my own fortune-telling cards. I got a lot of craft paper and cut out **twelveteen** rectangles. Then I gave them fancy king and queen names like Star's cards. I couldn't remember the

exact titles, but I knew each card was about something very **specifical**.
I made some up that sounded very perfect. Queen of Spectacles. King of Quiet. Prince of Friends and so on.

When I was done, I shuffled them all together and tied a rubber band around them so they wouldn't spill out.

I went to my mom's closet and chose a red scarf that looked very similar to Star's to tie around my head. Then I opened the linen closet and picked a tablecloth that was very colorful because that is what Star's tablecloth looked like.

What I really needed was a crystal ball. I know Star didn't have one, but that's because she isn't the kind of fortune-teller who looks inside a crystal ball. It is a scientific fact that I *am* that kind of fortune-teller.

Then my brain remembered an old **brain note** about something. Elliott's mother loved to bowl so much she owned her own bowling ball! A bowling ball is the exact shape and size of the crystal ball I imagined in my head!

I stood very still for a minute to see if my eyeballs felt like they were fortune-telling eyeballs. When I decided they were, I called Elliott and asked if I could borrow his mother's bowling ball.

While I did not have a red dress exactly, I decided I would wear something red, **however and nevertheless**. It is against the law for fortune-tellers to wear any other color except red.

I laid out my red pants, my red short-sleeved shirt, and my purple long-sleeved shirt on the chair to wear the next day. That was my **worker outfit**. If my business went very well, I would probably have to wear this outfit every day.

Then I went down to the living room where there were a **thousandy** leftover fortune cookies and brought them up to my room. My mom said I could bring them to school to share with everyone.

When I was done gathering everything, I spent a little time practicing my skills. My dad walked by me in the kitchen, and I said, "Dad. Today you will not encounter any obstacles."

He stopped, smiled, and said, "Bird, I hope you are right."

"At the end of the day, will you tell me if I was?" I asked him.

"It's a deal."

When I saw my mom I said, "Mom, today you will hear from a faraway relative."

"I didn't know I had any!" my mom said, **surprisified**.

I didn't know if she had any, either.

"Well, you will," I told her. "I see it in your future."

Then I went outside to watch my dad mow the lawn to see if he encountered any obstacles. He did not.

My mom came outside, too, and when he saw us, he waved and then called out for some iced tea because that's his favorite. The phone did not ring once, so I was disappointed that my powers about a faraway relative were wrong.

At dinner that night, my dad told me that he did not encounter one obstacle that day. My fortune-telling powers were very strong.

"Actually, they are only *half* strong," I told him. "I told Mom that she would hear from a faraway relative, and she didn't."

"Yes, she did," my dad said.

My mom and I looked at each other

with **quizzical** eyeballs.

"I called out to Mom for some iced tea when I was mowing the lawn. I was far away, *and* I'm a relative."

"Oh yeah!" I said, smiling. "That must be what I meant!"

I swelled up with **pride-itity**. That fortune cookie was right. I *was* a natural at this. I was very happy to know that my powers were in tip-top shape to open my very own business.

I was so excitified to open my fortune-telling business at school the next day that I got into bed an hour early. Tomorrow would come much sooner that way, but that is not certainly how it felt. I was actually very **boredified**. Eventually, though, I boredified myself to sleep.

CHAPTER

When I woke up, it was with the hugest fortune-telling smile. I was so **excitified**, I could even feel a grin underneath my smile. I'm very smart about under-smile grins. I ran downstairs and raced through breakfast.

Then I got dressed faster than anyone ever has in the world, jumped into the backseat of the car, and tried to make my mom drive faster **with my**

brain. I think it worked a little bit.

When we got to school, my mom kissed me good-bye and I ran inside, up the stairs, and into the cubby room to get the crystal ball from Elliott. He wasn't there yet, so I sat inside my cubby and waited. I waited so long, my head almost fell off.

Finally, after I thought I was going to have to walk to his house and get him myself, Elliott showed up. He was lugging the heaviest-looking bag in one hand, and his backpack was falling off his shoulder.

"Here's the bowling ball, Frannie," Elliott told me, dropping it with a crashing thud right at my feet. "It's very heavy."

"Thank you so much, Elliott. I didn't realize it would be so heavy. I'll carry it from now on," I told him because that was only fair.

Then I unzipped it to see if maybe it accidentally turned into a crystal ball. But it hadn't. It was still just a regular, old bowling ball. It was white, though, not black like most bowling balls. This was **good news** to me because it meant that I would have an easier time seeing inside of it. I put it in my cubby, and when Millicent and Elizabeth arrived and were putting their coats away, I told them that I was starting a fortune-telling business and they could be my first customers.

"Where are you going to open it?" Elizabeth asked me.

"The cafeteria," I said. I needed a very big space to hold all my customers. I could have also used the gym since it was bigger, but it was also squeakier and smellier. That would not be good for business.

On our way to our classroom I started to worry about how many things I had to do to set up my business, actually. First of all, I needed a sign. And a table. And a chair. This was not all stuff I could do by myself. And then, **you will not even believe your ears** about this: All three of my friends, Elliott, Millicent, AND Elizabeth, asked if they could work at my fortune-telling company.

The second they asked me, I got **tingly top skin** about something. Star told me I'd be the boss of at least three people, and here I was . . . being the boss of THREE PEOPLE. I could not believe how amazing a fortune-teller she was. This meant that they were supposed to be my workers and not my customers, which is a for instance of why I told them yes.

However and nevertheless, the first order of business was to have a meeting.

Meetings are very important, and my dad has them from time to time. He has to shuffle a lot of papers around to get ready for them, and he always puts the papers in his briefcase. Briefcases are **extremely official**, so I knew that if you say you're going to have a meeting, it's very **seriousal** and honestly professional.

That is why I said we would have a meeting. It would be an extremely fast meeting after class. They agreed, and then we all rushed into our seats before

Mrs. Pellington yelled our faces off for being late.

Mrs. Pellington had been telling us all about the map of the United States. She had a pull-down poster and a long stick she used to point to the different states.

I decided to use this time to practice fortune-telling. Every time Mrs. P. would lift her pointer from one state, I would guess which state she'd go to next before she got there. (It is not an opinion that I was right a lot of the time, and those are the times I felt very fortune-tellerish.)

Then I fortune-told that Millicent would secretly be reading a book on her lap, and when I looked over, she was turning the page of a book she was secretly reading on her lap. Millicent was always secretly reading books, but that does not mean I didn't fortune-tell it.

When I looked over at Elliott, he was doodling on the map Mrs. Pellington asked us to draw. I knew he'd be doodling!

I could not wait to open my business already. All this sitting around was wasting my superpowers of fortune-telling.

When recess came, **I was twenty-hundred years and forty-five minutes old**. That's how much time passed before we could get to work setting up my business. Since we had lunch right after recess, it gave us time to plan.

At my school we have indoor and outdoor recess. There is a playground right outside the cafeteria, and you have your choice of where you want to spend the half hour.

Because we had to have an **official meeting**, we stayed inside. I've never heard about adults having professional meetings on a playground.

In our meeting we decided to open the business in the cafeteria at lunchtime. Then we decided we would use the lunch table we were sitting at as the fortune-telling table.

I asked Elizabeth to make a sign. She had the best handwriting, which is a for instance of why I asked her.

She asked Mrs. P. if she could get craft paper and glitter pens from the art room and Mrs. P. said yes, if she was fast about it. Millicent was in charge of carrying the supply bag, which was where my scarf, cards, and tablecloth were. And I was **in charge** of the crystal bowling ball.

While Elizabeth was busy getting the craft paper, I reached into the supply bag and pulled out my scarf and wrapped it around my head. That's when I remembered the fortune cookies!

I asked Mrs. P. if I could run back to the classroom and get something from my cubby. She said yes, but just be fast about it. It is a scientific fact that I was faster than Elizabeth.

When I got back with the fortune cookies, I unzipped Elliott's mother's bag and pulled out the white bowling ball, which I put right on top of the tablecloth, in the center of the table.

Soon, Elizabeth came running down from the art room holding a scroll of red paper. When she unscrolled it, I could not believe my **eye sockets** about how beautiful it was. It said FREE FORTUNES FROM FRANKLY with bright-green glitter glue. It was one of the most amazingest signs I'd ever seen.

I made a **brain note** to remember that Elizabeth was an excellent sign maker. If I ever opened a sign shop, she would be the first person I'd hire. She and Elliott taped it to the front of the table.

Just then, the bell rang. Recess was over and lunch had started. "We are officially open for business," I announced.

Then we watched as kids streamed into the cafeteria for lunch. Once kids started to sit down with their trays, I told Elizabeth, Millicent, and Elliott that they could get to work. But they all looked at one another **confusified**. That is when I realized I hadn't told them *how* it worked!

"One of you has to go and pick the exact right person to get their fortunes told," I explained.

They all looked at one another. Who would it be?

"You could take turns," I suggested.

"Can I go first?" Elliott asked.

Free
Fortunes
From Frankly

I looked at the others who seemed not to mind.

"Sure."

"How will I know who to pick?" Elliott asked. That is when I remembered what Star had told me. "You will feel it deep inside your guts."

Then Elliott ran off to find our first customer, and Millicent and Elizabeth stood there not knowing what to do.

I told them they should stand at the long table with me, but they should not **speak** or **hover**.

"Pay close attention, just in case you ever have to take over my business."

They sat down just as Elliott brought over my first customer. It was an older boy I had seen but didn't know. Elliott knew him because they were both in the music recital.

"This is Ben. You will now tell him his fortune," Elliott said and then stood behind me to watch everything.

"Hello, Ben," I said. "I will now start your official reading."

"Okay," he said.

"Would you like your palm read, your cards told, or to hear about your future from the inside of this crystal ball?" I asked him.

"Palm," he said, and stuck his arm out at me.

This made me **a little bit upset** because I really wanted to use the crystal ball.

"Are you sure?" I asked. "What about the crystal ball?"

"What crystal ball?" he asked.

"This one," I said, pointing to the bowling ball.

"That's not a crystal ball. That's a bowling ball," he told me.

I did not appreciate that at all.

Ben stuck his hand out. "Palm," he said.

I was not **actually** certain that I liked my first customer very much, and that is not an opinion.

CHAPTER

If Ben could not see that the bowling ball was actually a crystal ball when it was on the fortune-telling table, he **obviously** did not have a very good imagination. And if he didn't have a good imagination, he was probably very boring, indeed.

I looked at Ben's very boring hand. I couldn't remember the names for all the lines. I realized that even if I did, I didn't know which line was which.

I held Ben's palm and looked at it very carefully. Then I lifted my head.

"What is your question?" I asked.

"I don't have a question. I just want to know about my life," he said. I looked back at his palm.

"It's very boring," I told him.

"Boring?" he asked, offendified.

"Yes. You don't have too much imagination. If you get more imagination, you will have a better life."

"How do I do that?" he asked.

I looked back down. "Be more interesting."

"Can you tell me anything else about my life?" he wanted to know.

I looked at all the runny lines. "You are going to get married and have six kids and make over one hundred dollars a month."

Ben looked very **impresstified** with his life.

"You don't have a health line, which is a good thing. It means you will never get sick."

"Thank you!" Ben said, extremely **happified** by his reading. "You are a really good fortune-teller," he said.

"Thank you very much," I said, and then I leaned over and pulled a fortune cookie out of the bag. I stood up and he stood up, and when I handed the cookie to him, I said, "This concludes our reading."

He took the fortune cookie and walked away very pleased with my natural ability.

Millicent brought me a girl who wanted her cards read. Her name was Valerie. While she was shuffling the cards, a few kids walked over to see what was going on. Elliott shushed them because he knew I needed my **concentration** in order to tell a really good fortune.

"Please think of your question," I said.

"I have not been doing well in math class," she said. "Will I get better at it?"

"That is a very excellent question," I said. "Please put the cards down."

Valerie's face was **mashed up** tight, and she was staring very hard at the cards. I picked up the top card and turned it over. It was the Queen of Spectacles. Then I turned over another card: the King of the Sun. I looked up at the girl. She looked up at me, and she looked very worried and **smashed up** her face even tighter.

"You are having trouble seeing the blackboard," I told her. This made perfect sense because of how **squeezed up** she was making her face.

"No," she answered. "I see it just fine."

"Apparently and nevertheless you do not see it fine. This card is the card about glasses, and it means that you need them because you can't see well. That is why you are doing badly in math. This card means if you look right at the sun you might go blind. So don't look at the sun. Please turn over another card."

Valerie turned over another. It was the King of Fours.

"Yes, you need glasses. This is a four, and it means you need four eyes in order to see well. You have only two eyes. Tell your parents you need glasses immediately. Until then, do not raise your hand in any classes. You are not seeing the board right. The words that are written are different words than what you see. If you participate in class, you will be embarrassed. You have broken eyeballs, and they need to be fixed," I told her. "You might as well just sit in the back row." More people had gathered around.

"Now that you mention it, sometimes things *do* seem a little blurry," she told me.

"Probably more things than you realize. This is a very serious problem, and you will not do well in school until it has been corrected," I said. "Do not take any tests or write anything down. You will get everything wrong until you get glasses." Then I reached into my bag, pulled out a fortune cookie, and stood. "This concludes our reading."

When I looked up, I saw that there were kids standing around me. That was when people started yelling,

"Me next! Me next!"

Millicent brought over her friend Katy. Katy chose the cards, too. She didn't get the Queen of Spectacles, but she did get the Prince of Trouble. I told her she better not say another word the entire day. That was the only way to stay out of trouble. If she talked, she'd definitely be punished.

Elizabeth chose a boy in Elliott's music class. His name was Eric, and I did not like him very much because he was **a big show-off**. He told Elliott that he was better at clarinet, and that is not a scientific fact. Besides, he doesn't even play clarinet. He plays trumpet.

Eric chose the crystal ball.

"Please ask me a question, and I will look inside to your future and tell you your answer."

"Will I get a standing ovation tomorrow at the concert?" he asked.

"You mean will everyone get a standing ovation?" I asked him, since it was a group playing, not just Eric.

"No, I mean just me. Out of everyone in the brass section, I play the best, so I am the one people should stand and ovate for."

I put my hands on the bowling ball, and everyone was **chattering** to see what I'd say. The chattering was making it hard to concentrate, so I turned toward the crowd.

"Please be quiet. I am trying to fortune-tell," I told everyone. They all went quiet right away.

I put my hands back on the bowling ball and looked inside of it. There was nothing actually that I could see, but I could see how much I did not like Eric's question. It was very **unsharing** of him.

"Something is going to happen tomorrow night in the brass section," I began.

"What do you mean?" Eric asked me, leaning forward.

"Shhhhh . . . ," I said, shutting my eyes. In my imagination, I taught him a lesson. I saw exactly what I hoped would happen, even though I knew it couldn't.

"When you blow into your trumpet, no sound will come out of it. In fact, no one in the brass section's instruments will work. Only the woodwind instruments will work," I told him. Elliott was in the woodwind section.

"Really? What should we do about that?"

"There is nothing you can do," I told him.

"Should we take our instruments apart and see if we can fix them before that happens?"

"I suppose, but that will not help."

"The whole brass section, you say?" Eric asked.

"The whole brass section," I said, feeling very powerful indeed. When I turned to look, there was an **actual real-life** crowd of people waiting to get their fortunes told. This was the best business I'd ever run!

CHAPTER

After a few more fortunes, I was getting a bit tired and also hungry. I hadn't even eaten lunch yet, so I was also just a little cranky when Solomon sat down. Solomon was very **slobby**. He never cleaned up after himself, and he always left his lunch tray on the table instead of clearing it. He wanted his palm read.

"What is your question?"

"Will I have to do chores for the rest

of my life?" he asked. When I looked at his palm, it was very dirty. All the lines were filled up with dirt.

"Your hands are very dirty. This means that you always make a big mess," I told him.

"I DO always make a big mess! Wow, you are really good at this."

I looked back down at his palm again. I was very hungry and was **not in the mood** for more fortunes. I knew that Solomon was never going to be a clean person, no matter what. That is why I told him what I did.

"Because it is so dirty, that means you will never have to clean up again, ever. You can stop doing it right now because no matter what, you will never be clean. You don't even have to take a bath or a shower ever again because your lines are telling me that your whole life is going to be dirty."

Solomon was so happy about this news, he almost hugged me, but he did not.

Everyone was so happy with all my fortunes, I knew that nothing could go wrong.

Then I handed Solomon a fortune cookie and said, "This concludes our reading."

Then Millicent, Elliott, Elizabeth, and I ate our lunches faster than anyone in the entire world. The bell rang when we were still eating, so we decided to leave my office there and come back later to clean it up.

When we were rushing to our classroom, some older kids waved, and one of them called out to me, "Hey,

Frannie—am I going to get a good grade on my geography test?"

I **could not believe** older kids knew my name and also were asking me for their fortunes!

"Yes. You will get a very high grade, indeed and nevertheless," I called out.

I was so **impresstified** with myself. I really didn't know I'd be so good at this, but I really was. I was almost geniusal. So geniusal I thought that I should keep my business open all week. The rest of the day was smooth sailing.

When I got home, I decided to make even more cards. I didn't want to use up the exact same fortunes on everyone. The new ones I made were so fantastical, I could hardly wait to use them on people tomorrow.

While I was doing my homework at home that evening, the phone started to ring itself right off its neck.

"Frannie, it's for you. Someone named Solomon."

I picked up the kitchen phone. "Hi, Solomon."

"Frankly, I don't like the fortune you gave me," he said.

This was very **shocktifying**. Solomon had been so happy with his reading. He said that I was right about him being messy.

"Why not?" I asked.

"My father says I have to take a bath no matter what. He said no ifs, ands, or buts. You said I never had to bathe again, but I do!"

This was a bit **stumpifying**. I did not know why something like this would happen when we both agreed about what right a fortune I gave him. That is why I told Solomon to pretend to take a bath.

"Go into the bathroom, turn on the water, and read a book until enough bath time has passed."

"Good idea. Thanks, Frannie."

When I hung up, the phone rang again and my mom called out, "It's Katy, Frannie!"

"Can I speak now?"

"You haven't been speaking all this time?" I asked a little surprisified.

"No, you told me not to."

I liked being the fortune-teller for the school. I did not want the fortunes to come to an end. That is why I told Katy she should **keep on not speaking**.

"If you do talk, you will get into trouble," I explained.

"What about tomorrow?" she asked.

"You have to stop talking until the fortune wears off."

"Well, when's that?"

"I don't know. I'll just feel it in my guts, and then I'll let you know."

"All right, but it's almost dinnertime, and my parents like to hear about my day."

"Just nod your head, but do not speak. No matter what!" Then I hung up the phone on her because I didn't want her to speak anymore. Not even to say good-bye.

As I headed to the kitchen for dinner, the phone rang one more time. My mom answered it and told me it was Valerie.

I couldn't believe how many kids from school were calling me about their fortunes. I was getting very exasperated.

"Hello?" I asked with just a smidge of annoyance.

"Frankly?"

"Yes?"

"This is Valerie."

"Hi, Valerie."

"Mr. Leonard said we are going to have a quiz tomorrow. What should I do? I have to take it."

"Do not take that test, Valerie," I told her. "You got the Queen of Spectacles. The cards do not lie. Your eye sockets are broken, and you will fail the pop quiz if you take it. I repeat, do not take that test."

"So what do I do?"

"Go to the nurse and say you don't feel well."

"That's really smart. Thanks, Frankly!"

"You're welcome."

Finally the phone stopped ringing, and it was dinnertime. That was when my mom told my dad that the phone had been ringing its neck off, and our house felt like a regular office center. That was music to my ears. I was filled to the absolute **toppest** part of my head with the feeling of being a boss. It was one of the best feelings I'd ever had in my **worldwide** life.

CHAPTER

The next day before lunch, Elliott took me aside and told me he was feeling **very nervous** about the concert. He asked if I could tell him his fortune really quickly. He wanted his palm read. I looked at Elliott's palm, and it looked **very good**, indeed.

"Elliott, you are going to have the best life," I told him.

"I am?" he asked.

"Yes. You are going to be a very

famous musician, and tonight when you play, everyone in the audience is going to clap the very hardest for you."

"Really?"

"Yes, that is what I see, and my eye sockets do not lie."

"So I won't mess up?"

"Not even a centimeter. You will be the best clarinet player there."

Elliott was very happy about this news and walked away with the **hugest** smile on his face.

I had a lot of new customers, so it was very **psychic** of me to have made more cards. I was also very glad no one said anything to me about wearing the same red outfit two days in a row.

Evan wanted me to use the cards to tell him if his father was going to take him to Florida for spring break. Last year, Evan was a big **secret spreader**, and that was something I did not appreciate about him. I don't know if he ever learned his lesson, but I do know that some kids STILL don't talk to him. That's how much he told other people's secrets. If there is one thing I know, it's that secrets are to be kept and not spread!

When he turned the first card over, I knew that I had something very important to tell him.

"Evan, you got the Friend card."

"What does that mean?" he asked. "Am I going to Florida?"

"This is not about Florida. This is about something else. Something much bigger," I told him.

"What?"

"One of your friends is telling a secret about you."

"But I don't have any secrets."

"Well, then it is a rumor. Someone is spreading a rumor about you."

"My friends wouldn't do that to me."

"This card is the Friend card, and that is what it means. You cannot argue with the cards. They do not lie. I am telling you for a scientific fact that your friends are all telling secrets or lies about you."

"All of them? I thought you said just one," Evan said.

I couldn't remember what I said, but it didn't matter, really. The **news was bad** no matter how many friends were telling secrets.

"It is all of them. You better find out who it is and get them to stop. Otherwise, you don't want to be friends with them anymore. This concludes our reading," I told him, giving him a fortune cookie.

Evan did not look very happy when he walked away. I felt bad about that, but I was just doing my job.

Paige got the card of Sickness so I told her that she better watch out for symptoms.

"What kind of symptoms?" she asked, worrified.

"It can be anything," I told her. "Just pay very close attention to your body today. If you get pins and needles, you should go to the nurse. If you feel any stomach pain, go to the nurse."

"I don't feel any of those things now," she said.

"Maybe not now," I told her. "But you will soon."

"Are there other symptoms I need to watch out for?" she asked, bringing her hand to her neck. "Sore throat? Headache?" she asked.

"Maybe, but make sure no hairs fall out of your head. This is very bad news. Also, if you get a ringing in your ear, you should go to the nurse. If you get dizzy or feel your legs growing really tall, go to the nurse. This concludes our reading," I told her.

Paige walked away **very lightly and slowly**, just so she wouldn't get sick. I had time for one more person before I had to eat my own lunch.

Elizabeth wanted her fortune told so I made her the very last person. You will not even **believe your ears** about this. Elizabeth got the exact same card as Paige. I told her all the very same things. Elizabeth did not look very well when we were done. I told her that it was already happening. I could see the sickness on her face.

CHAPTER

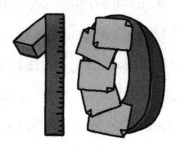

During class with Mrs. Pellington, Elizabeth raised her hand and told Mrs. P. she didn't feel well. Mrs. P. sent her down to the nurse. I was **very glad** that Elizabeth was taking her fortune seriously.

After class, I saw Paige holding her stomach, and then she put her hand on her head to check for a fever. She probably wasn't a very good fever checker because she asked another kid to check, too, and when he did, he shrugged like he didn't know.

It was a very good thing she saw me when she did. I went over to her and felt her head, and it was burning hot. I told her she had to go to the nurse before **her head fell off**. She took me very seriously, too, because she ran down the stairs toward the nurse's office.

On my way to art class, I saw that Evan was yelling at someone. I could hear him saying, "I know it was you. Tell me why you are spreading lies about me!"

The kid he yelled at burst into tears and said he hadn't said anything. That was when Evan turned to another kid and pointed his finger at him.

"It's you, then! You are telling lies about me!"

"No, I'm not! That's not a very friendship thing to say to me," the friend said before storming off.

I **scooched** away fast and was passing a classroom when the door swung open, almost hitting me in the face. Katy was walking out of the classroom with tears streaming down her face. Mr. Hirsch was very upset.

"I bet you will find your voice when you are sitting across from the principal, Ms. McLarney."

I passed the principal, who was talking to Mrs. Benedict, and overheard him ask, "Have you seen Mark? He left early yesterday, and I haven't seen him at all today."

Uh-oh. I had told Mark he was going to be a millionaire and probably never needed to come to school again.

I was starting to get a **very bad day feeling on my skin**. I decided that I would just leave it alone and everything would sort itself out. I would not fortune-tell for the rest of the day.

I had art class, which meant I'd see Solomon. I would tell him that he could take a bath today. That way, he wouldn't get into trouble and I'd be **saving the day**.

When I reached the art room he was already there, but he didn't even look up when I walked in.

"Hi, Solomon," I called. "I'm glad I found you."

He looked up at me, and my stomach dropped a bit when he saw my face. "I am not glad to see you."

"Why not?" I asked. I did not like when people were not glad to see me.

"I got in big trouble because of you," he told me.

"You did?" I asked.

"Yes! You told me not to shower, and I got in trouble. Then you told me to pretend-shower, but my parents could smell that I was not clean, and I got into even bigger trouble. Now I am grounded because of you."

"Sorry, Solomon. I didn't know that would happen."

"Then you're not a very good fortune-teller, are you?"

"I am, too, a very good fortune-teller. I just told you what the cards told me!"

"I don't care. If you were a real psychic, you would have seen that I was going to get grounded."

"Well, I told other people the right fortunes," I said.

"Humph, we'll see about that," he said. "It's still early."

I did not appreciate that Solomon did not believe in my **powers**. I felt very bad that he got into trouble, but that was the fault of the cards he picked, not my fortune-telling skills.

All the other kids started to stream in to art class, and I went to sit next to Solomon, but he got up and moved away, which hurt my feelings **very deep down inside**.

CHAPTER 11

The rest of the school day was better than in the art room with Solomon. No one else complained or got in trouble, so I started to feel a little bit better. Besides, I couldn't be in a bad mood because tonight was the big recital! I could not wait to see how amazing Elliott was going to be.

My mom and dad were coming to the recital, too. So we had a very early dinner, then changed into concert clothes and headed off to the school. I loved coming to school at night because you weren't expected to do any hard work at night.

When we got there, the place was filling up with parents and teachers. I could hear some musical instruments way in the deep end of the school **blurting** and **blaring** out their warm-up sounds. The lights flickered on and off, which meant it was time to get in our seats.

My parents and I sat with Elliott's mom. She was with my dad's friend George! My mom had told me that they met at the party and were getting to be really good friends.

The band was sitting in all their seats, but the stage seemed emptier for some reason. That's when I saw that the entire brass section was missing.

My stomach **frogged up** and **down** because that's when I remembered about my fortune to Eric. I hoped that the brass section was just late. But not on account of my telling Eric that none of the horns would make a sound. The woodwinds were practicing, and Elliott saw us and waved, and we waved back.

The lights went out, and then they went back up again suddenly. People started fidgeting, and then finally Mrs. Wiley came out onstage.

"Ladies and gentlemen, I am so sorry for the holdup. It seems there's been a little misunderstanding with the brass section. For some reason the kids had it in their heads that their instruments were broken and they've taken them all apart. We have been furiously assembling the instruments, but we could use some volunteers. If anyone is good at assembling brass instruments, please come backstage and we can get going."

A few people got up out of their seats and went backstage.

"That's one of the strangest things I've ever heard," my dad said. "Why would they all take their instruments apart?"

"Mrs. Wiley said they thought their instruments were broken," my mom told him.

"But that doesn't add up. Why would ALL the kids think the entire brass section wasn't going to work?"

My mom **squinched** her face up and said, "You're right. That *is* strange."

I sat as still as possible and did not move one muscle of my mouth or say one single word at all. Finally, after what felt like **five school years**, the adults came back to the audience.

When the brass section came out, the audience gave a big clapping shout of *hurrahs!* I looked at Eric, and he seemed very nervous. Not like his normal "I am better than everyone else in the world" self.

Then Mrs. Wiley stood in front of them and started to conduct. Everyone lifted up their instruments and started to play, except for Eric. The other kids in the band started looking at him and whispering to him, but he just sat there and quietly shook his head no.

I wished right then that I could disappear into the **smallest molecule of dots**. That's how terrible I felt about telling Eric his instrument wouldn't play. That's how terrible I was starting to feel about the fortunes I told everyone.

The entire concert came and went, and Eric didn't pick up his instrument once. When it was over, everyone clapped so hard, they stood up and kept clapping. A standing ovation! I was right after all!

In the lobby afterward, Eric's parents were standing over him, and I could tell they were very upset. That's when he saw me and pointed. His parents looked over and my parents looked over, and they exchanged questioning looks.

"Who are those people, and why are they pointing at you?" my mom asked.

"That's Eric, and those are his

parents. I might be in a little bit of trouble, actually and as a matter of fact," I said, just as Eric and his parents came to stand right next to us.

"Hi there. I'm Lydia Cooper and this is Dave Cooper," Eric's mom said to my parents. "It seems your daughter might have given our son the idea that no matter what he did, his instrument would not play tonight and he just shouldn't bother."

My parents looked at me, and I felt my face glow the brightest red, like in Star's dress.

"Is that true, Frannie?" my mom asked me. "Why would you say something like that?"

"It wasn't my fault. It was his fortune!" I explained.

"His fortune?" my dad asked.

"She opened a fortune-telling business at school," Eric said in a sort of tattlish way.

"You did what?" my mom asked.

"I opened a fortune-telling business. I'm very good at it, too."

"But you don't know how to tell people's fortunes, Frannie."

"Sure, I do!" I said. "I was Star's assistant!"

"But she studied how to do it for years. You studied it for an hour. That does not make you an expert."

That was not a good day feeling kind of sentence.

"I'm very sorry about this," my mom said to Eric's parents. "We will certainly find a way for Frannie to make this up to you."

Then they smiled and said good-bye, and my dad said, "We're going to have a good, long talk about this when we get home, Frances."

I knew I was in big trouble because he Frances-ed me.

On our way to find Elliott, I saw Mark and his parents, who were scanning the room for someone. When they saw me, they did not look away. Instead, they started to walk in my direction, and that is when I knew actually and certainly that I was about to be in the biggest trouble of ever.

CHAPTER

"Hi," Mark's mom said. "I'm so sorry
to bother you, but are you Frankly?"
she asked me and my parents. We all
shook our heads yes. Even though I
knew I was going to get in trouble, my
heart grew the **biggest smile** when
she called me Frankly.

"It seems your daughter has
convinced our son he doesn't need to
show up to school anymore."

"I don't!" Mark said. "I'm going to be

a millionaire. I don't even *need* school!"

My parents' faces were the most furiousal I'd ever seen them.

"Oh, Mark, I'm sorry to tell you that Frannie made up those fortunes. She doesn't *really* know how to tell fortunes," my mom explained. Mark's face almost fell off his face, and I felt a little maddish that my mom was telling him this.

After they walked away, my parents said I had to find every kid whose fortune I told and tell them the truth.

"Right now?" I asked.

"I see no better time," my dad stated. "Everyone is here. You just need to find them. So let's go."

And that is what we had to do. We walked around until I found Katy and Valerie and Paige and Elizabeth and Solomon and everyone else whose fortunes I pretended to tell.

I told them that just because I told the fortunes did not mean the fortunes were true. In fact, the **fortunes were not true at all**, even if they felt true. I was very sorry if I made bad things happen. I thought I was going to be a natural, but maybe I was not.

I must have been a very **convincible** fortune-teller because it took a **foreverteen** amount of years to convince everyone that their fortunes were not going to come true. I had to admit out loud that I was not actually a fortune-teller. After I apologized **my entire face off**, we could finally go home.

I felt a **big relief off my chest**, but I also felt a little bit bad that I hadn't thought the whole thing through.

My fortunes were so good, I didn't think that anything could possibly go wrong. Star's fortunes were good and hers didn't go wrong. But my parents reminded me that I am not an actual fortune-teller and Star is.

When we got in the car, I breathed a sigh of relief.

"I'm glad that's over," I said.

"What's over?" my mom asked.

"The fortune-telling trouble. I'm glad I got all my apologies over with. Now I feel much better."

"Good. I like when you are in tip-top shape to deal with the consequences of your actions."

I sat up really **strict** and **tallish**.

"The consequences? But I just apologized to everyone."

"Sorry is not always enough."

"What is my consequence going to be?" I asked.

"Well, since you caused trouble on school grounds, I think it's up to the school to punish you."

"The school?" I could not even believe my ears about this terrible news.

"Mrs. Pellington in particular. I'll call her in the morning and tell her she has been hired for the job."

I was not excited to go to school the next day. Not one bit at all.

CHAPTER

I woke up with the most **horrendimous** feeling on my skin. I was not excited about Mrs. Pellington's punishment. It was probably going to be something really **schoolish**, but not in a workerish kind of way.

A for instance of what I mean is that she would probably make me wash the entire school from head to toe. Or she might make me teach every single class at the exact same time, which seemed like a very impossible thing to do.

However and nevertheless, none of those things were my punishment. The first order of business she told me was to take down my business and officially close the shop. I could not get any help from anyone, and I had to do it during recess. I returned the bowling ball back to Elliott's cubby and threw out the empty bag that once had all the fortune cookies. Then I went back to our classroom.

"Frances, I have decided that you will be eating your lunch here every day for the next week," Mrs. Pellington told me.

"By myself?!"

"Yes. It will give you plenty of time to consider all the other career options that are not fortune-telling."

"But I was a very good fortune-teller, Mrs. Pellington. Everyone said so," I told her.

"Maybe they said so at first, but it sure didn't turn out well for everyone in the end, did it?"

I looked at my shoes. "I guess not."

"I'll go and get your lunch for you. Stay right where you are and think about all the things you told everyone and how your words affected other people's actions."

"Okay," I told her.

Mrs. Pellington walked to the door and then stopped and turned around.

"Frannie?"

"Yes?" I asked, hoping she might be changing her mind about my punishment.

"If you are such a good fortune-teller, why didn't you know you were going to get into trouble?"

I looked up at Mrs. Pellington who smiled at me and walked away, leaving me alone in the classroom **stumpified** about that question.

I had to admit that perhaps maybe I wasn't as good a fortune-teller as I thought I was. Or maybe even as good as I wanted to be, but I was very good at making cards. I guess sometimes I forget that not everything I think up is true. Even Star told me that I get caught up in my own fantasies.

And that's when I realized that Star had been right with each of her fortunes for me. But I had been wrong with every fortune I told.

Maybe Mrs. Pellington was right. It was time to think of a new career.

Fortune-telling was not my **strong suit**.

That is why I walked over to the trash can and threw my cards out. It was time for me to consider a **new line of work**.

THE END.

Will Frannie ever land that perfect job?

Here's a sneak peek at her next try:

FRANKLY, FRANNIE

Rocking Out!

by AJ Stern

illustrated by Doreen Mulryan Marts

"Aimee Chapman!" I blurted out.

My parents stopped talking. Elliott stopped talking, and they all looked at me.

"Aimee Chapman," my dad said like it was a statement type of sentence.

"Aimee Chapman," my mom said in a "that is the most geniusal idea I've ever heard in my worldwide life" voice.

"Aimee Chapman," Elliott said in his "I cannot believe that my best friend is the smartest person who was ever born on this planet" voice.

Aimee Chapman was a very famous singer who even had songs in movies. She was a grown-up type of singer, but she was **funnish**, so everyone loved her—kids and adults. She wore stylish clothes like swirly-colored scarves and hats with feathers in them and blazers that were too big for her. They made her look sometimes like she was going to an office. That was one of my favorite parts about her, outside of her songs which I really loved and knew all the words to. I've seen pictures of her, and she even carries her guitar in a guitar type of briefcase. That made me feel like we would be very good friends and be **understandable** of each other.

Aimee Chapman was the right person for the job of saving Noah's Ark. We all felt that way. That was why after dinner, my parents, Elliott, and I jumped into the car and drove over to the Ark to tell Noah. We all ran to the front door and even though all the lights were out, we knocked.

"Come on, Noah!" I said out loud. "Please be inside."

We knocked again.

When we were convinced he'd gone home for the day, we headed back to the car, and just then, Noah opened the door!

"Noah!" I called.

"Frannie!" he called back.

Elliott and I ran to the door, and my parents followed us.

"What's going on?" he asked.

That's when I looked at him, and in my most **seriousal** and professional voice of ever I said, "Aimee Chapman."

Then he broke out into a very handsome smile, nodded his head yes, and said her name like it was the **cure for all the problems on earth**.

We knocked again.

When we were convinced he'd gone home for the day, we headed back to the car, and just then, Noah opened the door!

"Noah!" I called.

"Frannie!" he called back.

Elliott and I ran to the door, and my parents followed us.

"What's going on?" he asked.

That's when I looked at him, and in my most **seriousal** and professional voice of ever I said, "Aimee Chapman."

Then he broke out into a very handsome smile, nodded his head yes, and said her name like it was the **cure for all the problems on earth**.

blazers that were too big for her. They made her look sometimes like she was going to an office. That was one of my favorite parts about her, outside of her songs which I really loved and knew all the words to. I've seen pictures of her, and she even carries her guitar in a guitar type of briefcase. That made me feel like we would be very good friends and be **understandable** of each other.

Aimee Chapman was the right person for the job of saving Noah's Ark. We all felt that way. That was why after dinner, my parents, Elliott, and I jumped into the car and drove over to the Ark to tell Noah. We all ran to the front door and even though all the lights were out, we knocked.

"Come on, Noah!" I said out loud. "Please be inside."

Want more Frannie?

Check Out All the Books in the Series Including

Frankly, Frannie: Rocking Out!
Coming Soon!

When Frannie's local recreation center announces that it's going out of business, Frannie and her friends join together to create a fund-raising concert! Being a rock star is the perfect career . . . or is it?

Visit FranklyFrannie.com

- Make your own business cards and résumé
- Write a very official letter
- Make your own sock doll
- Take a quiz to find out your perfect job
- Read all about Frannie's books
  ...and more!